Mary's Little Lamb

AND MORE FARM FUN RHYMES

Illustrated by
KRISTA BRAUCKMANN-TOWNS
JANE CHAMBLESS WRIGHT
WENDY EDELSON
JUDITH DUFOUR LOVE
ANITA NELSON
LORI NELSON FIELD
DEBBIE PINKNEY
KAREN PRITCHETT

PUBLICATIONS INTERNATIONAL, LTD.

MARY HAD A LITTLE LAMB

Mary had a little lamb,
    Its fleece was white as snow.
And everywhere that Mary went
    The lamb was sure to go.

HARVESTING

The boughs do shake
    And the bells do ring,
So merrily comes our harvest in,
    Our harvest in, our harvest in,
So merrily comes our harvest in.

We've plowed, we've sowed,
    We've reaped, we've mowed,
We've got our harvest in!

My Maid Mary

My maid Mary,
   She minds the dairy,
While I go a-hoeing
   And mowing each morn.
Gaily runs the reel
   And the spinning wheel,
While I am singing
   And mowing my corn.

CUSHY COW

Cushy cow, bonny, let down your milk,
    And I will give you a gown of silk.
A gown of silk and a silver tee,
    If you will let down your milk to me.

YOUNG LAMBS

If I'd as much money as I could tell,
    I never would cry young lambs to sell.
Young lambs to sell, young lambs to sell,
    I never would cry young lambs to sell.

COCK-A-DOODLE-DOO

Cock-a-doodle-doo,
  My dame has lost her shoe,
And master's lost his fiddling stick,
  Sing doodle-doodle-doo.

Shave a Pig

Barber, barber, shave a pig,
   How many hairs will make a wig?
Four-and-twenty, that's enough.
   Give the barber a pinch of snuff.

A Dozen Eggs

I bought a dozen new-laid eggs
    From good old Farmer Dickens.
I hobbled home upon two legs
    And found them full of chickens.

Baa, Baa, Black Sheep

Baa, baa, black sheep,
    Have you any wool?
Yes, sir, yes, sir,
    Three bags full:
One for the master,
    One for the dame,
One for the little boy
    Who lives down the lane.

THE LEARNED PIG

My learned friend and neighbor pig,
  Odds bobs and bills, and dash my wig!
It's said that you the weather know.
  Please tell me when the wind will blow.

THE BOY IN THE BARN

A little boy went into a barn,
  And lay down on some hay.
An owl came out and flew about,
  And the little boy ran away.